This Book Belongs To:

....

CONTENTS

Nutwood Winter Sports...............Endpaper
Rupert and the Flavours 4
Rupert's Paper Tortoise 25
Rupert and the Mixed Magic 26
Rupert's Cat Search 44
Rupert's Secret Route 45
Rupert and the Blizzard.........................46
Rupert's Memory Test............................71
Rupert and the Ocean Office...............72

RUPERT

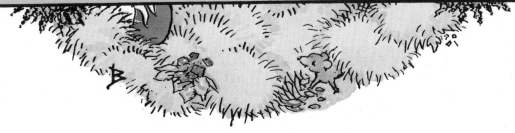

A DAILY EXPRESS PUBLICATION

ISBN 0 85079 096 4

£1.60

RUPERT

*"Just see that dark cloud over there!
It's going to pour soon, I declare!"*

One winter's day Rupert coaxes his chum Podgy Pig to go for a country walk. Although he is not keen, Podgy agrees. But he soon starts to complain and when he sees a dark cloud loom up he stops. "It's going to rain," he says, glad to find an excuse. "I knew we shouldn't have come. Let's go back." Just then the rain begins and as large drops patter down, Rupert calls out: "There's a barn. Let's run for it!"

and the FLAVOURS

"Let's shelter!" Rupert tells his chum
Who cries, "I wish we hadn't come!"

Mouth open, Podgy lies down flat.
Gasps Rupert, "What's he playing at?"

Rupert dashes ahead and gets to the barn first. "Oh, what a downpour!" he pants. "Still, I don't think it will last . . ." He swings round to find that Podgy is no longer with him. Then to his dismay he sees his chum lying on his back in the rain with his mouth wide open. "Oh, he must have hurt himself," Rupert thinks and, throwing an old piece of sacking over his shoulders for protection from the rain, he runs to help Podgy.

"Is Podgy hurt?" He dons a sack
To keep him dry then hurries back.

Says Podgy as he smacks his lips,
"This rain taste just like fish and chips!"

"You can't lie here! You're getting wet!
We'll dash for shelter. Up you get!"

"That rain was flavoured like I said.
Try some." But Rupert shakes his head.

A voice, when it is fine again,
Asks, "What did you think of the rain?"

"Podgy! Are you hurt?" Rupert asks anxiously as he reaches his chum. But the little pig sits up and says brightly, "Of course not. I was having a drink of this lovely rain. It tastes just like fish and chips!" Rupert looks hard at Podgy and says, "Come on, stop fooling. You'll be soaked if you stay out here." Podgy starts to say, "I mean it . . ." But Rupert pulls him to his feet and, covering his shoulders with the sacking, leads him to the barn. Once the pals are under cover Podgy says, "It's

true. The rain really does taste like fish and chips. Try it yourself." But before Rupert can answer, the rain stops and at almost the same moment a voice behind them says, "Well, my little friends, what did you think of the rain, eh?" And the chums turn to find the tall, quiet man they know as The Inventor. "I've been keeping an eye on you," he smiles. Rupert wonders what the man meant about the rain, particularly just after what Podgy has said about it.

RUPERT TASTES THE RAIN

*"What Podgy told you was no lie
The rain is tasty. Have a try!"*

*So Rupert tries a few small sips.
"You're right! It tastes of fish and chips!"*

*"Yes, I can make rain taste of fish
Or any other food I wish."*

*"Ice cream and toffee apples, too,
Just right for plumpish folk like you."*

"I came out to catch a sample of the rain," The Inventor explains. "I designed this just for the job," he adds, showing the pals the odd umbrella he is carrying. They can see that he has indeed collected rainwater in the upturned brim. "When I saw one of you lying in the rain with his mouth open I guessed the flavour had been discovered. You, little bear, didn't believe your friend so you'd both better try it." And he holds the odd umbrella low so that the two pals can dip their fingers in the water and taste it. "Why, it does taste just like fish and chips!" exclaims Rupert. "But how . . .?" The Inventor chuckles quietly. "I put the flavour into the rain," he says. "Indeed, I can make the rain any flavour I choose. It's my latest idea." "Even ice-cream and toffees?" asks Podgy with shining eyes. "Anything at all," says The Inventor. "It's just the thing for plump folk like you." And he prods Podgy. "Now if you will come with me I'll see how much you weigh."

RUPERT IS ASKED TO HELP

"My rain, instead of too much food,
Would keep folk slim and still taste good."

"I shan't weigh Rupert since he's slim.
I have a special job for him."

"I pump up flavours which are sprayed
On rainclouds from this mast I've made."

"Empty the brolly, please, with care,
While I weigh Podgy, little bear."

On the way The Inventor tells the chums about his plans. "If only people would drink my tasty rainwater instead of eating so much," he declares, "they'd stay slim." "Will you want to weigh both of us?" asks Rupert. The Inventor gives him the umbrella to carry. "No," he replies. "Only your friend. You're slim enough. But there is one thing you can do for me. I've heard that you are good at climbing." Just then they arrive at The Inventor's house. Beside it stands a girder mast stretching up to the sky. "This mast," says The Inventor, "has a sprinkler at the top. I pump up whichever flavour I choose and spray it on to the rain clouds. The liquid comes from this big tank here." Then telling Rupert to empty the umbrella into a bucket, he leads Podgy off to be weighed. As he empties the umbrella Rupert wonders what sort of job The Inventor has for him. "He said it had something to do with climbing," muses the little bear. "What could it be?"

RUPERT IS TOLD HIS TASK

The speak-your-weight machine's voice shakes,
"T-twenty tons . . . crrrang!" Then breaks!

"You're far too heavy, that's well seen!
You've ruined my brand new machine!"

"I've tried to climb the mast but felt
Too dizzy. Use this safety belt."

"For you must climb the mast and seek
The spot that drips and seal the leak."

Rupert empties the sample of rainwater into the bucket and carries it into the house in time to see Podgy step on to a weighing machine. "Keep perfectly still," The Inventor is saying, "and it will speak your weight. It switches itself on." There is a click then a spluttering voice comes from a loudspeaker. "T-twenty tons . . . sptzz! . . . burr! . . . ping! . . . five grammes . . . eighty pounds . . . crrrang!" The Inventor drags Podgy off the machine. "You're so heavy you've damaged it!"

he exclaims. The Inventor strides around the room looking cross. "It is most upsetting when things go wrong!" Then he stops and peers at Rupert. "Ah yes! That climbing job!" He opens a big box and takes out a belt with a chain attached. "Put this on for safety. You'll be going very high." The little bear is puzzled. "But where am I going?" he asks. "Why, up the mast to find a leak in the flavours pipe and mend it," The Inventor replies. "I'd go, but heights make me dizzy."

Some tubes marked "Flavours" Podgy spies,
And samples one. "Yumm-yumm!" he cries.

"Stop! Stop! One sip is flavour for
Five hundred puddings—even more!"

"You'll have to take this antidote!"
A dose is poured down Podgy's throat.

"Now, little bear, it's starting time.
A thousand feet you'll have to climb!"

"I am quite sure the leak is near the top of the mast," The Inventor explains to Rupert. "And it must be sealed as soon as possible." While he is talking Podgy wanders off into the next room. He spots a row of tubes marked "Flavours". What a chance to try them, he thinks, and putting one to his mouth, takes a swig. "Yumm! Scrumptious!" he murmurs. Just then The Inventor sees what Podgy is up to and darts in to snatch the tube from him. "Foolish thing!" he shouts. "That is extra strong essence. One sip is equal to five hundred whole chocolate puddings!" Hurriedly he produces a big bottle and makes Podgy take a spoonful from it. "This will take away the effect," he says. And though Podgy shudders and squirms, he has to take several doses. By the time The Inventor leads Rupert out to the mast Podgy is feeling very sorry for himself. Rupert peers up the tall mast. "How high must I climb?" he asks. "A thousand feet," is the reply.

RUPERT CLIMBS THE MAST

Poor Rupert pleads, with quaking knees,
"Oh, couldn't someone else go, please?"

Making sure the chain is fast,
Rupert starts to scale the mast.

"So high, and still can't see the top!
Ah, there's the leak that I must stop."

"Make sure that this repair patch sticks.
I hope that it's not hard to fix."

The thought of having to climb so high fills the little bear with alarm. A thousand feet! "Isn't there anyone else who could do this for you?" he asks, pausing on the ladder. "But of course not," replies The Inventor irritably. "I wouldn't ask you otherwise. You don't expect your plump chum to go up, do you?" Plucking up his courage and taking a deep breath, Rupert starts to climb the mast, hooking the safety chain above him every few rungs. After a while he stops and looks at the ground far below. "I don't like this at all," he thinks. The climb seems endless and he can't see the top of the mast which is hidden in the clouds. Then he spots a small hole in the pipe beside the mast. "That must be the leak The Inventor spoke of," he thinks. He takes the repair patch from the pouch The Inventor has given him and examines the hole. To reach it he has to lean right out at the end of the safety chain. "If . . . if I should fall now. . ." he thinks with a shudder.

RUPERT IS GIVEN A MESSAGE

"I've reached the flavour-sprinkler! Whew!
A bird is perching on it, too!"

The bird caws loudly, "You down there,
Explain this monstrous thing, young bear!"

"Flavour the rain! Our pure supply
Of drinking water! Let him try!"

"You warn that foolish flavours man,
We'll take revenge and foil his plan!"

Taking care not to look down, Rupert soon fixes the sticky patch over the hole in the pipe then takes a firm hold on the ladder again. Suddenly the clouds part and he sees that he is near the top of the high mast. "That tube at the top with holes in it must be The Inventor's sprinkler for spraying the clouds with flavours. I say, there's a big bird perched on it!" Just then the bird spots Rupert. "Come up here, little bear!" it caws loudly. Carefully Rupert makes his way to the top. "What is the meaning of this thing?" demands the bird. Clinging to the mast, Rupert tries to explain to the bird about The Inventor's ideas. "How dare he!" squawks the bird. "All we Nutwood birds depend on the rain for our drinking water. We don't want his horrid flavours." It wheels angrily round the mast then returns and cries: "Warn the man that unless he stops spoiling the rain we birds will take our revenge." And with that it flies off towards the distant woods.

RUPERT PASSES ON A WARNING

Now Rupert's anxious to descend
And take the warning to his friend.

"Bah! Those birds protest in vain!
They'll soon get used to flavoured rain."

"More rain forecast. No time to lose!
Which flavour would you like to choose?"

And as the chums head home again
Podgy gloats about fruity rain.

Rupert is keener than ever to get back to the ground again. But the journey down the mast is slow for he has to fasten and unfasten his safety chain every few steps. At length he reaches the bottom to be met by The Inventor and Podgy. He tells the man that he has repaired the pipe then goes on to repeat the bird's warning. But The Inventor is scornful. "Bah! What can birds do?" he scoffs. "My plan is far too important to be stopped now. They'll get used to the flavours in time." He stalks back to his house followed by the pals. "I must be ready for the next spell of rain," he mutters, studying a barometer. "I see it's becoming colder and we shall have more rain. I must prepare another flavour. What shall it be this time, eh?" "Oh, please, fruit salad!" Podgy pleads. "Good idea," muses The Inventor. "Fruit salad it shall be." On the way home the little pig talks about nothing else. "Well, just don't lie in it this time!" laughs Rupert.

RUPERT HELPS PODGY'S PLAN

"Mummy's been cooking—what a spread!
Still, I'll wait for that rain instead."

"I tried a Flavour and somehow
I'm not the least bit hungry now."

"Help me," pleads Podgy, then the chums
Fetch bowls for when the rainfall comes.

"Spread all of them across this plot
Then I shall catch a lovely lot!"

When the pals reach Podgy's home the little pig invites Rupert to stay a while. "Mummy's been cooking," whispers Podgy, gazing at the goodies spread out on the table. "It's just a snack for you, Podgy," smiles Mrs. Pig. But the little pig won't touch a morsel. "I tasted some stuff at The Inventor's house," he explains, "and I'm not very hungry now." "Yes, it was all part of an idea for flavouring rain," chimes in Rupert. And the pals start to describe their adventure, but Mrs. Pig soon gives up trying to make any sense of it. "I can't spare any more time," she declares. As she returns to her work, Podgy collects as many big bowls as he can find. "Come on, Rupert, give me a hand," he asks. "I'm going to set these out to collect that fruit salad rain when it comes. I shall have a wonderful time!" And although Rupert smiles and shakes his head at Podgy's greediness, he joins in and together they begin to spread the bowls all over the lawn.

RUPERT TELLS HIS DADDY

"Hi, Daddy!" Rupert gives a yell.
"I have the strangest thing to tell!"

"That puddle's flavoured too, you'll find!"
"What! I'll do nothing of the kind!"

"Brr-rr! It's freezing!" Mummy says
And stirs the fire into a blaze.

"Rupert, wake up! The world's all white!
We've had a snowfall in the night."

After helping Podgy, Rupert sets off for home. On the way he sees his Daddy just ahead of him. "Hullo, Daddy, you'll never guess the adventure I've had!" he cries. And as they stroll along he tells Mr. Bear everything that has taken place at The Inventor's house. But Mr. Bear treats it as just another of Rupert's rambling tales. "Rain that tastes of fish and chips! You're pulling my leg!" he says. "Truly I'm not," insists the little bear. "Even that puddle over there on the road is flavoured." "I don't think I'll taste it anyway," grins Daddy. Later that evening Mrs. Bear stirs the fire to a blaze. "It's turning really cold," she says. "Perhaps we shall have snow." At the word "snow" Rupert looks up from his book. He remembers The Inventor's plans and wonders if the snow will be flavoured too. Then he thinks, "Perhaps it won't really snow." But next morning Daddy wakes him early. "Look! We've had a heavy fall of snow," he announces.

RUPERT GOES TO HELP

"You're right! This snow does have a taste!"
Then Rupert cries, "No time to waste!"

"It's frozen—ponds and rivers too!
Whatever will the poor birds do?"

"I'd better find those birds. I think
They won't like flavoured snow to drink,"

"Fruit-flavoured snowballs do taste nice!
Much better than vanilla ice."

Snow! At once Rupert is wide awake. His Daddy scoops a handful of snow off the window-sill. "Up you get!" he laughs. "Now you really will be able to have some fun!" As he turns to go Rupert asks, "Does that snow in your hand have any taste?" Mr. Bear repeats, "Taste?" But he puts it to his lips and tries. "Yes, it has!" he exclaims, amazed. "Like . . . fruit salad!" And he recalls Rupert's adventure of the day before. Later in the garden they find the bird bath is frozen solid. "All the streams and ponds will be frozen too," Rupert says worriedly. "What will the birds do?" Then still worrying he sets out to find some of the Nutwood birds. "They peck snow when there's no drinking water," he thinks, "but they will hate the taste of this flavoured stuff!" Just then he meets his pal with an armful of snowballs. "Can't stop to play, Podgy," Rupert begins. But Podgy grunts and says, "Don't want to play. I've made these snowballs to eat. They taste just like fruit salad!"

But Rupert presses quickly on.
"One bird! Where have the others gone?"

"Too thirsty now to fly or sing,
They've gathered by our secret spring."

"Come, follow me," the bird cries. "Please!"
And leads the way into the trees.

"Our secret pool is frozen thick.
We cannot break it. Help us, quick!"

Leaving Podgy to gloat over his flavoured snowballs, Rupert presses on towards the woods. There is a strange hush everywhere as he plods through the snow, and the birds are not in their usual haunts. At last Rupert sees one hunched miserably on a branch. "Where are all your friends?" asks Rupert anxiously. "I've come to see if you need drinking water." "Yes, we do," replies the bird. "When times are hard we rely on our secret spring of water. But now we can't even drink from

that." Rupert looks so dismayed that the bird says, "See for yourself if you like. I'll show you the way." With an effort the bird rises and flutters ahead of Rupert. "Keep in sight," it calls. And soon Rupert is being led through parts of the wood he has never seen before. At last they reach a tiny pool hidden among rocks. Unhappy looking birds are gathered round the frozen water. "This is our secret spring," says Rupert's guide. "But the ice is so thick we can't break it."

RUPERT CANNOT BREAK THE ICE

"With snow we cannot quench our thirst.
This horrid flavour's quite the worst!"

He hits the ice with might and main,
But Rupert's efforts are in vain.

"How can we wait until the thaw?
It's that man's fault!" the poor birds caw.

"We'll make him sorry! What a waste
To give pure rain that nasty taste!"

At first the birds are wary of Rupert, but when they learn that he has come to try to help them they all cluster around him, chattering at once. "We've had nothing to drink since the icy weather began," chirps one. "And we can't peck the snow because it tastes so horrid," pipes another. "And now our spring of pure water is frozen solid," a blackbird adds. "Perhaps I can break the ice on your spring," suggests Rupert. But although he hammers the ice hard with a piece of rock it is too solid for him. "It's no use, I'm afraid," he pants. "I can't crack it." There is an angry sort of murmuring among the birds around the pool. "It is all the fault of that man," one of them chirps. "Our scout found he was sprinkling stuff on the clouds to give the rain the kind of flavours that people like." "Yes," agrees Rupert. "First fish and chips. Now fruit salad." Suddenly the birds begin to swarm around Rupert. "Revenge!" they cry angrily. "We'll make that man sorry! Revenge!"

RUPERT WARNS THE INVENTOR

The birds take off in vengeful crowds
And fill the sky like angry clouds.

"This snow experiment's my best.
And now to do a flavour test."

"The birds are angry! Please take care!"
Blurts out the anxious little bear.

Now birds crowd on the window sill,
Angry, screeching, wild and shrill!

The birds sweep past Rupert and soar above the trees, still screeching their anger. "I wonder what they mean to do," Rupert worries. "Maybe I'd better let The Inventor know." Retracing his own footprints in the snow, Rupert makes his way out of the wood. As he hurries towards the house of The Inventor the sky is streaked with clouds of birds gathering from all quarters. Rupert finds The Inventor filling a pail with snow. "Hello," he says. "I wasn't expecting you. I'm taking this snow in to test its flavour . . ." "Please!" Rupert interrupts. "The birds are terribly angry because you flavoured the rain. Hundreds of them are coming here for their revenge!" "Rubbish!" snorts The Inventor. "They can't harm me. You're making a fuss over nothing. Now come and watch me test this snqw." But Rupert is very uneasy as he follows The Inventor indoors. When they reach the workroom birds are already starting to flutter against the windows.

RUPERT PLEADS WITH THE BIRDS

The window's dark with screaming birds.
The noise! Too terrible for words!

"Stop! I give in! I'll end my tests.
Please make them go back to their nests!"

Rupert runs out to tell the crowd
Of birds, "You've won! Don't screech so loud!"

"He says he wants you all to know
No more he'll flavour rain or snow!"

Even as Rupert and The Inventor watch, the birds grow in numbers until the windows are darkened by them. The noise of their angry screeching fills the room. "Oh, I can't stand this!" The Inventor cries. "It's terrible. Stop! Stop!" But still the noise goes on and on until at last, looking pale and frightened, The Inventor turns to Rupert. "I give in!" he shouts above the uproar. "Make them stop and I'll promise never to experiment with rain again!"

"I'll tell them at once!" cries Rupert and he dashes outside and scrambles up the stairs that lead to the flat roof. When the birds see him they swarm up from the windows, circling angrily. Rupert waves his arms and calls loudly, "Birds! You've won!" The birds stop wheeling in order to hear Rupert. "You've won!" he repeats. "The Inventor begs you to stop. He says that if you leave him in peace he promises never to put any sort of stuff in the rain again!"

RUPERT ASKS FOR MEDICINE

"I think they're waiting, every bird,
To make sure that you keep your word."

Now The Inventor, moving fast,
Makes straight towards the giant mast.

"We'll add this liquid to make sure
The snow that's due is once more pure."

"Save me a little of that stuff,"
Begs Rupert, "when you've used enough."

Now the birds are all silent. But they watch Rupert as he makes his way back to The Inventor. The little bear hopes that they have understood his message. Inside the workroom again he tells The Inventor, "I think they understand and that they are waiting to see what you'll do." "Yes, I must show them that I intend to keep my promise," says the man. "I couldn't stand any more noise." Then he picks up a bottle. It is the one he used to dose Podgy when the little pig drank the strong essence. "I'll put this in the sprinkler. It'll take away the flavour of the snow." Carefully he pours the stuff from the bottle into the tank as the birds watch in silence. "I can't sprinkle it until the next fall of snow," he adds. "But there is more due very soon." Suddenly Rupert remembers something. "Can you save a little of that stuff?" he asks. "I shall need it later." "Of course," says the surprised Inventor. "You may have what is left now. But why do you want it?"

RUPERT'S PAL FEELS UNWELL

"Podgy may need another dose,"
He tells the man and off he goes.

The bird squawks, "He means well, we think.
But just the same, what can we drink?"

"Fruit salad snowballs!" Podgy moans.
"They've given me tummy-ache!" he groans.

"Come on!" says Rupert. "Get this down!
Oh, yes, you must! No use to frown."

Rupert points towards the village. "On the way here I met my friend Podgy," he explains. "He was about to have a feast of flavoured snowballs and I'm afraid he might make himself ill. So I need some of this stuff, just in case." The Inventor nods. "Most thoughtful of you," he says. "And if you get the chance tell the birds that the next fall of snow will dissolve the flavour of the last fall." So Rupert sets off with the bottle and he has not gone far when some birds swoop down beside him. When they hear what he has to say one of them cheeps, "That's all very well but what do we drink in the meantime?" Rupert is still trying to think of an answer when he spies Podgy propped up against a tree. "Oooo! I've such a tummy-ache," he wails. "I ate too many of those fruit salad snowballs." "I thought so," says Rupert. "Lucky for you The Inventor gave me what was left of this stuff." "Oh, not that again!" begs Podgy. But Rupert makes him drink it.

RUPERT GETS A CALLER

The special cure works like a charm
And Podgy's led away from harm.

"You leave those snowballs where they are!
Now, home we go! It isn't far!"

Now Rupert's Mummy hears him tell
How with the snow all will be well.

A scrumptious meal awaits the pair.
Then comes a knock! "I'll see who's there!"

Although Podgy splutters and complains all the time Rupert is making him swallow The Inventor's cure, he is soon feeling well again. "Good, then let's go home," says Rupert. Even now Podgy can't resist a glance back at the snowballs he has left behind. "Seems such a waste . . ." he begins, but Rupert takes hold of his arm. "No, you are not going back for them. You'd only make yourself ill again!" And still holding Podgy's arm firmly, he marches him homewards.

At home Rupert has lots to tell his Mummy, but his story leaves her quite bewildered. "So, you see, everything will be put right with the next fall of snow," he ends. "Well, that's amazing!" gasps Mrs. Bear. "But don't leave Podgy out there, Rupert. Ask him in for lunch." The little pig's appetite has returned and as he starts on a large bowl of soup he chuckles, "Real food's best after all." Just then there is a knock at the front door. "I'll go, Mummy," Rupert says.

RUPERT MELTS THE ICE

*It's The Inventor come to bring
Some powder. "Now the birds can sing!"*

*"A little powder on the ice
Will melt the thickest in a trice."*

*One pinch, and where the ice has been,
Pure water, crystal clear, is seen.*

*The first bird drinks and starts to sing.
"Next," laugh the chums, "the secret spring!"*

Rupert opens the door to find The Inventor. "I have called to give you this," he says and hands Rupert a small box. "After you'd gone I recalled a powder I once invented for turning ice back into water. This is it and I thought you'd like it to keep the birds happy until the snow comes." "Oh, thank you!" exclaims Rupert. "It's just what they need!" Podgy joins him in time to see the man at the gate and to hear him call, "Just sprinkle a little on the ice. It works very quickly."

As soon as Rupert and Podgy have finished their lunch they hurry out to the bird-bath which is still frozen hard. "This will make a good test," Rupert says, sprinkling some of the powder on the ice. In just a few moments the ice melts. "The birds will be so happy!" laughs Podgy. "Yes, and this afternoon I'm going to use it on the bird's secret spring in the woods," says Rupert. "Come on let's both go. We can tell them this is The Inventor's way of saying he's sorry."

RUPERT'S PAPER TORTOISE

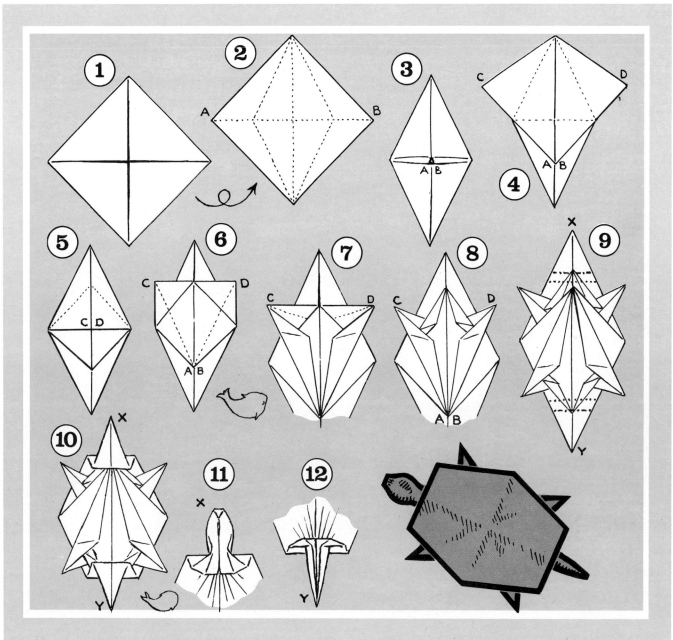

After several tries Tigerlily taught Rupert to make this paper tortoise. For it you need a piece of thin, strong paper at least six inches across. Fold it from side to side each way to find the centre then fold all four corners to the centre as in Figure 1. Turn it over and fold each of the four sides in turn to the middle upright line to make the creases shown by the sloping lines in Fig 2. Using these creases, press all four sides as far as possible down on the middle line, leaving points A and B standing up as in Fig. 3. Fold A and B down and bring the loose flaps C and D out from behind as in Fig. 4. Fold C and D to the middle to form Fig. 5, then press these points back using the new dotted lines so that the sides from C to D make a straight line (Fig. 6). The next folds from A to C and B to D must end exactly at C and D to make Fig. 7. Now two rather tricky folds as you bring the short sides between C and D down to meet the upper edges of the new folds you have just made. To do this you will have to lift the upright middle edges a bit and press them over as in Fig. 8. This is to give you sharp points at C and D. Half your tortoise is now made. To finish it press A and B up the other way and treat the lower sides exactly as in Figs. 4 to 8. When you reach Fig. 9 bend the top point X down by the lower dotted line and back again by the upper one. Treat the lower point Y in the same way to get Fig. 10. The last two figures show how to narrow the neck (11) and the tail (12).

25

RUPERT and

The little Chinese girl has found
Three short rods lying on the ground.

Rupert is setting out to sail his new model submarine on Nutwood Pond when just outside the gate he sees his friend Tigerlily, the Chinese Conjurer's daughter. She is holding three short rods. "Hello, Rupert," she smiles. "I find these on path. One has little bell. Make lovely wand. Perhaps Daddy put some magic in it for me." Rupert takes the rods and examines them closely. "Look, they fit together," he says.

the MIXED MAGIC

"The three parts fit together. Look!
One fishing rod for line and hook!"

"The bell rings when a fish is caught.
Well—now the owner must be sought."

"It's a fishing rod, Tigerlily," says Rupert. "This reel thing on the handle is for winding up the line, and that little bell jingles when you've caught a fish. But it must belong to someone. I wonder who could have dropped it." "No one about when I found it," says Tigerlily solemnly. "Then you'd best look after it until we find the owner," suggests Rupert. "I shall mention it to my pals." And he makes off for the pond.

"You'd best look after it meanwhile.
I'm off," says Rupert with a smile.

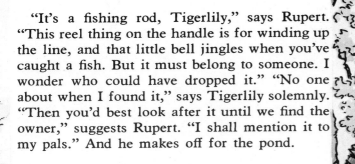

RUPERT'S PAL GETS A SHOCK

As Rupert winds his submarine
His best pal Bill comes on the scene

"I've come to do some fishing and—
Oh my, your submarine is grand!"

"My fishing rod! It's gone! Oh dear!
I must have dropped it coming here."

"My rod's been found, you mean to say?
I'll run and fetch it right away!"

Soon Rupert is at the edge of Nutwood Pond and winding up his new model submarine, ready to try it out. A sudden shout makes him look up to see his best chum, Bill Badger, hurrying towards him. "Fancy meeting you here!" exclaims Bill. "I've come for a day's fishing. What are you . . ." Then he catches sight of the submarine. "I say, is it yours?" he asks, gazing admiringly at the model as it moves across the water. "Yes, it's a present from my Uncle Bruno," Rupert replies.

"Good, then we'll keep each other company," smiles Bill, "just so long as your submarine doesn't frighten all the fish." As he speaks he is opening the flap of his haversack. Suddenly he gives a cry: "My rod! It's gone! I must have dropped it!" "Then that must be the one Tigerlily found," exclaims Rupert and tells Bill about his meeting with the Conjurer's daughter. "Oh good! Then I'll go and claim it at once," Bill cries and hurries off to find Tigerlily.

"My submarine's gone down, that's plain!
I do hope it comes up again!"

Rupert is trudging homeward, sad,
When Bill calls, "See what luck I've had!"

"The Conjurer—why, I can't tell—
Bought my rod and paid me well!"

Says Rupert, "Now, that's very odd!
Why should he want your fishing rod?"

Rupert turns from watching Bill hurry away and gives a gasp of dismay. All that's to be seen of his submarine are a few ripples where it has gone down. "Oh, I do hope it comes up again," Rupert murmurs. But although he waits and waits there is no sign of the model coming to the top. "I can't have wound it up enough," he sighs. "I suppose that means I've lost it for good." He turns sadly for home and on his way sees Bill coming back. "I say, I'm in luck," Bill calls. "Look at this!" He produces a bag of coins. "Tigerlily's Daddy, the Conjurer, wanted to keep my rod so he's given me this to buy a new one. There'll be enough for a fishing basket as well." But Bill's glee fades when he hears about Rupert's lost submarine and he tries to cheer up his chum. "Look, come and help me buy my fishing gear then we can share it for the day." Rupert agrees, but on the way he keeps wondering what the Chinese Conjurer can want with Bill's old fishing rod.

"*Since you can't stand a mystery,*"
Laughs Bill, "*you'd better go and see!*"

Smiles Tigerlily, "Why, it's you!
Yes, you can watch new magic too."

The Conjurer is muttering,
"*Mixed magic—daring thing!*"

"*So, Tigerlily, you bring chum.*
Will need you both. Glad Rupert come."

Bill can see that Rupert will not be satisfied until he has found out what the Conjurer means to do with the old rod. "You go and find out while I'm buying the fishing things," he chuckles. "We can meet later." So Rupert hurries off towards the pagoda house where the Conjurer lives. When he reaches it he finds Tigerlily putting shutters up at the windows and asks why. "My Daddy always want windows covered when he try new magic," she replies. "What sort of magic?" Rupert asks, but Tigerlily will only say, "Honourable Daddy keep ideas secret until he try them. But we watch if you very quiet." Excitedly Rupert promises and the little girl leads him indoors to where the Conjurer is getting ready in the shuttered room. On a table in front of him are the three parts of Bill's old rod. He is muttering, "It is daring to mix magic and I am first to try . . ." Then he looks up and sees the chums. "Ah, you bring your friend. Good! I shall need both of you."

RUPERT SEES THE MAGIC MIXED

*"Take one piece each, do just what told.
Different magic each shall hold."*

*"My piece can make things disappear!
Now, Rupert, please bring your piece here."*

*"Yours have power to make things shrink.
Last, topsy-turvy power, I think."*

*The Conjurer says, "Now that done,
Make wand, three magics mixed in one!"*

The Conjurer now shares out the rods. Tiger-lily gets the end with the handle, Rupert the middle part and the Conjurer keeps the rod with the bell. "I plan to put different kind of magic into each piece," he explains. "First mine. It shall have power to make things disappear." He sprinkles some glittering dust on the rod and Rupert steps back in alarm as the room fills with stars and flashes. "Not to be scared," whispers Tigerlily. "It very nearly over now." But Rupert is still just a bit nervous as the Conjurer turns to him and declares, "Middle piece you have shall have power to shrink things and your handle piece, Tigerlily, will be able to turn things topsy-turvy." He puts on his magic mittens and again stars and flashes light the room while he performs his magic. "Ooh! The magic's making me tingle," cries Rupert. At last all three rods are ready. Solemnly the Conjurer announces, "Now I mix the magic by fixing them together into one big wand!"

RUPERT GETS IN A TANGLE

"Hark! I hear flying saucer dive!
It land here! Sorcerer arrive!"

Now Tigerlily's on her own,
She cannot leave the rod alone.

"I chant spell," sings the little girl.
Then, whoosh! the whole room starts to swirl.

"This curtain!" Rupert gives a shout.
"It's wrapped around me! Get me out!"

Suddenly there is a roar of something passing over the house. "Hark, Daddy!" cries Tigerlily. "That sound like your friend the Sorcerer in his flying saucer!" Because the windows are shuttered they cannot see the surprise arrival, and looking puzzled, the Conjurer makes for the door, saying, "Not expect my friend. Why he come?" He hurries outside, leaving the wand on the table. "Oh, hope Daddy not long," Tigerlily says. "Want to know how magic work." "I'll see if they're coming," says Rupert, going towards the door. No sooner is his back turned than Tigerlily reaches out for the wand and waves it about, chanting magic words she has heard her Daddy use. At once the room swirls madly and furniture shoots about the floor. "Oh dear, what's happening?" cries Rupert hopping in alarm. Tigerlily gazes helplessly at the uproar. "Magic not go right!" she wails as Rupert tumbles over, caught up in a curtain. "Get me out!" he cries.

RUPERT IS TOLD HE MUST HELP

"Oh, naughty girl! What have you done?
That powerful magic not for fun!"

The Sorcerer says, "I've come to get,
I hope, the greatest magic yet!"

"Stay, daughter! You are in disgrace!
Rupert will have to take your place."

"I'll use the wand since you're so kind,
And Rupert's help if he won't mind?"

But before Tigerlily can rescue Rupert her Daddy returns with the Sorcerer. "Who has done this?" he cries as he frees Rupert from the curtain. His daughter bows her head. "So, it was you!" he says angrily. "You meddle with mixed magic and this is what happens!" As Rupert who is still rather shaky sits down to recover, the Sorcerer seizes the rod. "So this is the mixed magic wand!" he cries. "I came urgently seeking a wonder greater than all others. This surely is it!" "Then you must take it if your need is truly urgent," the Conjurer at once replies. "But be warned—it has not been tested!" As the Sorcerer thanks him and turns to go, Tigerlily starts to follow. "No!" her Daddy cries. "You are in disgrace for meddling with my magic." "But I hoped she might come as my helper," the Sorcerer says. The Conjurer shakes his head. "Then *you* must come instead, little bear!" says the other. And speechless with amazement, Rupert is led to the flying saucer.

RUPERT HEARS OF A CHALLENGE

The Sorcerer laughs as off they speed,
"This wondrous wand is what I need!"

"From this, his house upon the sea,
The Toti Wizard challenged me."

"There is no magic in the whole
Wide world that I cannot control!"

"Those statues are the Wizard's band
Of guards who leap to his command."

Held by a safety belt, Rupert clings to the old Sorcerer as the flying saucer takes off. "Where are we going?" he gasps as the craft wooshes out over the sea. "To the Wizard of Toti—my great rival," replies the Sorcerer. "He envies my skill and has challenged me to perform untried wonders. Now, thanks to this mixed magic wand, I shall be able to astound him!" Rupert is about to remind him that the wand has not been tested, when the Sorcerer points to a strange building on a sort of platform in the sea. "The Wizard's palace!" he cries. Soon they are climbing out of their craft at the end of a pier. The Sorcerer is confident. "In a child's hands this mixed magic wand might run wild. But I have the power to control it," he says. Rupert, however, is gazing in awe at the strange building. "Just look at those statues of animals!" he gasps. "They are not statues," the Sorcerer replies. "They are the Wizard's guard and will come alive at his bidding!"

RUPERT MEETS THE WIZARD

High on the Wizard's ocean home
They climb until they reach a dome.

"I meet your challenge! Let me in!
Or do you fear that I shall win?"

They enter, through a sliding door,
A room with magic things galore.

"So you have come to face my test,"
The Wizard cries, "and prove you're best?"

Rupert doesn't like the sound of carved animals that can come to life. And the whole place seems eerie. There is no one about and he can see no way of getting into the palace. When he says so the Sorcerer tells him to be patient and leads him up a long flight of steps. "The Wizard is a very careful man and protects himself well," explains Rupert's companion. When they reach the big dome the Sorcerer calls out loudly: "Open up! I would have audience with the Wizard!"

Immediately part of the dome opens moving to one side slowly and silently. "So this is the way in. Just like a secret panel," whispers Rupert. As they enter he nervously takes the Sorcerer's hand. The room they find themselves in is very large and richly decorated with symbols of magic. Rising to greet them, the Wizard smiles mockingly. "So you have come after all! Does that mean you have taken up my challenge? Have you brought me wonders that have never before been seen?"

RUPERT SEES THE MAGIC TRIED

"Well, Wizard, what then must I do
To prove I'm greater far than you?"

"Move from that cage the vase of gold!
That is the test!" the Sorcerer's told.

"With my new magic—WHOOSH!—I'll prove
The vase is easy to remove!"

Stars flash and frightening bangs are heard,
And everything by smoke is blurred.

"Yes, I have come prepared," the Sorcerer says. Proudly he produces the fishing rod. "This wand has powers beyond belief. What would you have me perform?" The Wizard smiles slyly and beckons his visitors towards a sort of cage. Inside it Rupert can see a large gleaming ornament on a pedestal. "That gold vase is my most precious treasure," the Wizard croaks. "If your wand can move it from the cage then you will have proved your greatness. I must tell you, though, that many other magicians have tried and failed." The Sorcerer smiles. "It shall be done!" he declares. He stands in front of the cage. "Stay close to me, little bear," he whispers. "There will be magic all around." So, nervously wondering what will happen, Rupert takes hold of his companion's robe. The Sorcerer swings the rod, chanting magic words. At once the room is filled with clouds of smoke, and stars explode with loud bangs. "Oh, I hope it's all right," quakes Rupert.

RUPERT IS TRAPPED

But, oh!, as stars and smoke subside,
The vase is free but they're inside!

"While you the cage's bars confine
I'll steal your magic, make it mine!"

"You still may use your magic arts,
Let's try the rod in separate parts."

"That seems a good idea to me!
Quick, get it unscrewed into three!"

At last the noise and smoke fade. And the gold vase is outside the cage. But—horror—Rupert and the Sorcerer are now inside the cage in its place! "What happened?" gasps Rupert. The Sorcerer groans. "I have blundered. The mixed magic was too strong for me and ran wild." Now the Wizard shuffles towards the cage. "Well done," he mocks. "You have freed my vase but at great cost to both of you. Now that you are my prisoner, Sorcerer, I shall go to China and ransack the secrets of your home. All your knowledge will be mine." And he leaves, cackling nastily. For a while Rupert and the Sorcerer say nothing. Then Rupert has an idea. "The magic in this wand is mixed up. But it might work if you try each part by itself. Let me see, there's disappearing magic in the piece with the bell. The middle bit has shrinking magic and the Conjurer gave the handle the power to make things topsy-turvy." At once the Sorcerer cheers up. "I have a feeling you may be right," he smiles.

RUPERT'S MAGIC IDEA WORKS

"The 'disappearing wand', let's see,
Should very quickly set us free!"

"I'm thankful that the wand obeyed,
But we're not safe yet, I'm afraid."

"Keep close to me. We'll make a dash!"
They reach the stone steps in a flash.

His magic carpet by the stairs,
The Wizard for his flight prepares.

Eagerly the Sorcerer takes up the piece of rod with the little bell on the end: "You say that this piece can make things disappear?" Rupert nods. "Good, then I shall try it first," says the Sorcerer. Drawing himself to his full height, he waves the little wand and commands the cage to be gone. At once there is a noise like thunder. The air quivers with flashes and clouds of vapour rise from the floor. "It's working!" exclaims Rupert. "Look! The cage has gone!" But the Sorcerer is already dashing towards the entrance. "Come on, hurry, little bear! We may still be in time to catch the Wizard!" Rupert races after him out of the dome. At the top of the stairs the Sorcerer stops. "There he is!" he hisses. Looking down, Rupert sees the Wizard unrolling a carpet. "That is his magic carpet," the Sorcerer whispers. "It will carry him to China and my home where all my secrets are kept. It would be terrible if he got all that power. We have little time to stop him."

RUPERT HAS ANOTHER IDEA

"Give me the rod that makes things shrink.
We'll stop him even now, I think."

"It will not work! We must get near!
But he might catch us then, I fear."

Then Rupert whispers, "Look, we can
Let down the rod and spoil his plan."

Just as the Wizard's set to go,
The shrink-power rod is dangled low.

Luckily for Rupert and his friend the Wizard is so intent on preparing his carpet that he does not notice them above him. "Quick, let me have that rod that makes things shrink," says the Sorcerer. With trembling fingers Rupert gives him the middle piece. At once the Sorcerer begins waving the rod towards the Wizard and uttering magic words. But nothing happens. "He's too far away for the magic to reach him," says the Sorcerer. "But if we go closer he will see us and put us under a spell of his own." The precious moments are slipping past, then suddenly Rupert has an idea. He attaches the handle to the rod with the bell. "Look, I've made a short fishing rod. We can use it to dangle the middle piece close to the Wizard." The Sorcerer at once acts on Rupert's suggestion, tying the middle rod to the fishing line then slowly unwinding the reel. Down goes the rod until it is level with the Wizard who is just about to start his flying carpet.

RUPERT AND HIS FRIEND FLEE

"This tiny carpet will not soar!
I'm foiled!" rings out the angry roar.

"Quick, Rupert! We must get away!
I fear he'll harm us if we stay."

"Seize them!" now hear the Wizard yell,
"Till I can hold them with a spell!"

Snarling, the Wizard's guard beasts bound.
Too late! The saucer's off the ground!

The Wizard is beginning to make magic signs over his carpet when the Sorcerer shouts a command and the dangling wand does its work instantly. The startled Wizard cries out in alarm as he sees his carpet shrink to the size of a doormat amid smoke and flashes. "Who has done this?" he roars. "I cannot travel on a carpet this size!" By now the Sorcerer and Rupert are down the steps and racing along the pier. "We'll soon be aboard the flying saucer!" pants Rupert. "We still have the Wizard to reckon with," replies his friend. Sure enough, they hear the Wizard cry, "Seize them, guards!" And the fearsome carved animals like huge dogs that Rupert had seen when he arrived, come alive. They leap down snarling and give chase, gaining on the friends with every bound. The Sorcerer is first aboard the saucer and works feverishly to start it. Then with the beasts on his heels, the little bear tumbles aboard. At that second the craft lifts clear of the snapping jaws.

RUPERT TRAVELS UPSIDE-DOWN

"The topsy-turvy wand, I think,
Will see the saucer does not sink!"

While upside-down the friends remain
The rain squalls lash their craft in vain.

"We're through the storm! I'll put things right,
So now you can enjoy the flight."

And now the Conjurer's home appears,
The end to danger, storms and fears.

"That was a narrow squeak!" gasps Rupert as the flying saucer speeds over the sea. But there is another danger ahead – a great bank of dark cloud. "We must go through it," the Sorcerer says. "But I fear the rain will fill the flying saucer and drive us into the sea." Then, just as the cloud looms over them, he says, "Quick, give me the bit of rod that turns things topsy-turvy!" Wondering, Rupert passes him the handle part. The Sorcerer takes it and utters a spell. At once the saucer turns upside down just as they enter the worst of the storm. As the rain batters harmlessly on the underside of the craft the Sorcerer cries, "Don't be frightened! Our safety straps will hold us." So with the upturned flying saucer warding off the rain like an umbrella they pass safely through the storm. "That was wonderful!" exclaims Rupert as the Sorcerer uses the wand to turn the craft right way up again. The rest of the way home is smooth and soon they spy the Conjurer's house.

RUPERT IS SAFELY HOME AGAIN

"My Daddy has forgiven me!"
Shouts Tigerlily in great glee.

And now the Sorcerer ends his tale:
"Mixing magic is sure to fail!"

"Then from this rod one part I'll choose
To make a wand young girl can use."

"Tomorrow we try special spell,
Change flowers' colours, who can tell?"

The Sorcerer makes a perfect landing beside the Conjurer's house and Tigerlily runs to meet them. "Daddy has forgiven me!" she laughs as she leads the friends indoors. The Conjurer's face grows serious as he hears all about their adventure. He nods as the Sorcerer says gravely, "Never again try to mix magic. It brings only trouble. But for this little bear's idea of using the three rods separately we would still be prisoners of the Wizard." "You are right," says the Conjurer. "I shall not try again." Then he takes the small rod with the bell and holds it inside a glass cabinet where it glows. "Daddy use box to change magic," Tigerlily whispers to Rupert. When the rod stops glowing the Conjurer hands it to Tigerlily with a smile: "A junior wand for you. It will perform simple magic and perhaps stop you meddling with mine." As Rupert is about to go Tigerlily says, "Come tomorrow and we try simple magic like changing colour of flowers."

RUPERT GETS A SURPRISE

There, in the same spot, fishing still,
Rupert comes on his best pal, Bill.

"I bought a fishing rod, brand-new!
And this big fishing-basket, too!"

"Just look! I've fished up something fine!"
"A submarine! Why, Bill, it's mine!"

In spite of that mixed magic spell,
Everything has turned out well!

Promising to call on Tigerlily next day, Rupert sets off for home. His way takes him alongside the Nutwood pond where he sees Bill Badger sitting fishing "Hello, Bill!" he cries. "So you've got your new rod! It's a fine one!" "That's not all I've got," laughs his pal. "I had enough money left over to buy this as well!" And he produces a brand new fishing basket. "That should hold a lot," says Rupert. "By the way, have you caught any fish yet?" Bill smiles: "Well, I have caught something, but you'd hardly call it a fish." And from his basket he brings out Rupert's submarine. "I hooked it out with my first cast. But if you want to try it again take my tip and tie it to the end of my fishing line. Then you can't lose it!" Delighted to have his submarine back, Rupert does as Bill suggests and soon the little craft is once more buzzing across the pond. "Now you sit down, Bill," says Rupert, "and I'll tell you all that's happened to me while I've been gone."

RUPERT'S CAT SEARCH

"I always come here to Cat Corner any time I feel lonely," says Dinkie the clever kitten. "When you're lonely?" Rupert repeats in amazement. "Of course," miaows Dinkie. "There's always plenty of company here." Rupert scratches his head. "Company?" he says. "For you? I simply don't understand." "Oh dear!" Dinkie sighs. "Why do you think it's called Cat Corner?" "I've sometimes wondered about that," replies the little bear. "Why is it?" Dinkie sighs again: "Because there are so many cats here, that's why. I can see lots right now. And so could you if you'd only use your eyes!" Well, how many can *you* see?

Answer on Page 71.

RUPERT'S SECRET ROUTE

"What a maze of fields and hedges there is between here and the windmill," sighs Bill Badger. Rupert laughs: "Ah, but I've found a secret route to get there. It's . . ." "No, please don't tell us!" interrupts Algy Pug. "Let Bill and I find it for ourselves." "Very well," says Rupert. "But you must remember not to go in the river and you must use only the gates and gaps in the hedges. What's more, the farmer says you mustn't go into any field with a notice board in it. Right? Then off you go!" And away scamper the other two. Algy goes over the bridge but Bill decides not to cross the water. Who finds Rupert's route?

Answer on Page 71.

Nutwood is in the grip of terrible storms. To save it Rupert must fly to a far-off land across the sea.

RUPERT SPIES AN OLD FRIEND

"There's something moving over there. What is it?" wonders Rupert Bear.

"Why, it's my friend, Jack Frost!" he cries. "Hi, Jack! This is a nice surprise!"

Rupert is excited and happy. It will soon be Christmas and he has been helping his Mummy to put up the decorations. But they have run short of holly and the little bear has gone up on to the common to find some more. It is a lovely bright day even though it is cold, and Rupert is glad to be in the open. Soon he finds a good bush with plenty of bright red berries, and he is starting to choose the best sprigs when something in the distance catches his eye. "Hello," he murmurs to himself, "I wonder who that can be." Whoever it is seems to be very interested in something and is staring hard at it. Then the figure turns a little and Rupert recognises him. "Why, it's my friend, Jack Frost!" he laughs. "So he's come to Nutwood, has he? No wonder the weather's as cold as it is!" And eager to greet Jack who is always pleasant, Rupert runs towards him.

the BLIZZARD

RUPERT'S FRIEND IS WORRIED

*"That Billy Blizzard means to start
A snow-storm! Here's his icy dart!"*

*"If we can't catch him it will mean
Such storms as you have never seen!"*

Jack Frost has just picked up something from the ground when Rupert comes up to him with a cheery greeting. But surprisingly, Jack who is usually a happy person does not smile. "Oh, it's you, is it, Rupert?" he says quietly. "Why, what's wrong, Jack?" asks the little bear. Jack holds up for Rupert to see a slender glassy thing rather like an arrow. "Do you know what this is?" he demands. "Why, no," Rupert replies. "I've never

seen one before. It's like ice. Look, it's beginning to melt. Is it important?" Jack heaves a big sigh. "It's an icicle dart," he declares. "And only one person uses them – my cousin Billy Blizzard. He was so troublesome King Frost just had to banish him. But this dart means that he is back again and that he has chosen Nutwood for one of his very worst snow storms. I simply must catch him! And you must help me, Rupert!"

RUPERT MEETS BILLY BLIZZARD

"And Santa Claus could not get through!
Oo—footprints! Could they be a clue?"

"Plotting against ME!" comes a shout,
"With Cousin Jack! What's this about?"

"You wait! I'll catch you, little bear!"
"Jack! Help me! Please!" But Jack's not there.

A hut! He's almost at the door!
Trips! And goes sprawling on the floor!

Jack Frost dashes off to start searching. But he has forgotten that Rupert doesn't know what his cousin Billy Blizzard looks like. "I suppose he forgot because he's worried," thinks Rupert. "So am I. If that Billy brings blizzards here Santa Claus won't be able to get through to Nutwood with our presents. I must start looking for any signs of Jack's cousin." Almost at once he spots some footprints and is just wondering if they might be Billy's when a figure jumps up from behind a rock. "I saw you plotting with Jack against me!" shouts the stranger. "What's your game?" Rupert knows at once that this is Billy Blizzard and he is so startled that he turns and bolts shouting, "Jack, help me!" Hard on Rupert's heels Billy screams, "Wait till I catch you!" Then ahead of him Rupert spies a hut with its door open and makes for it, hoping to get inside, shut the door and keep Billy at bay until Jack turns up. But on the threshold he stumbles and falls flat.

RUPERT AND JACK TRAP BILLY

Now Billy's turn to tumble, but
Rupert is up. The door's slammed shut!

Oh, how the hut door groans and creaks
While Billy hammers, kicks and shrieks.

Jack Frost arrives! "Quick, lean your weight!
You very nearly were too late!"

"Leave him to me. In there he'll stay
Or promise he'll go far away."

He is scrambling to his feet again when Billy catches up with him. But Jack's unpleasant cousin is going so fast that he can't stop and sprawls headlong over the little bear. With a wild shout of anger he lands inside the hut. And in that split second Rupert sees his chance. He leaps up and slams the door before Billy can get back on his feet. "Whew!" gasps Rupert leaning with all his weight against the door. Inside the hut Billy is hammering and kicking. "I'll make you pay for this!" he shrieks. Just then Jack Frost runs up. "I heard you calling, Rupert. What's wrong?" When he hears that Billy Blizzard is inside the hut, he throws his weight against the door. "I'll keep him in while you fasten the door!" he cries. Quickly Rupert slips a wooden bar into the slots. "Good! Now leave him to me," says Jack. "I'll see that he stays locked up until he promises to go away and stay away." So Rupert hurries off with Billy's shouts ringing in his ears.

Home with more holly Rupert goes.
Santa will get through now, he knows.

"Hooray! So Santa Claus has been!
Jack's banished Billy from the scene!"

It's warm and snug, and everyone
Is pulling crackers, having fun.

Then—brrr!—an icy gust sweeps through.
The winds shrieks! "My, it's snowing, too!"

Remembering to finish picking his holly on the way home, Rupert is soon indoors again. While he helps to decorate the Christmas tree he tells his Mummy and Daddy about Billy Blizzard. "It's lucky we trapped him when we did?" he says. "Wouldn't it be awful if his snow storm stopped Santa Claus coming?" "Indeed it would," smiles Mr. Bear. So the days pass. Nothing is heard from Jack Frost, and on Christmas morning Rupert wakens to find his presents waiting for him "Oh, Santa has been!" he laughs. "So Jack must have got Billy to leave Nutwood!" And soon Billy Blizzard is forgotten as Rupert settles down to enjoy the Christmas fun. He pulls crackers with his Mummy, then his Daddy helps him with a new jigsaw puzzle. Suddenly an icy draught sweeps through the cosy room. "Brr!" shivers Mr. Bear. "Did you feel that? I believe the weather is changing." Then Rupert hears the wind rising and the patter of snow on the window.

RUPERT'S FRIEND TURNS UP

Cries Rupert's Daddy, "What a night!"
And runs to shut the windows tight.

A knock! And Rupert finds Jack Frost
Trembling and weak and looking lost!

"It's—Billy—Blizzard—he—broke—free,"
Jack croaks. "Oh, Rupert! Please—help—me!"

"Mummy! Daddy! Oh, quick! Come here!
It's Jack! He can't stand up, I fear!"

At once Mr. Bear gets up to make sure that the windows are tightly fastened. But even now the wind is screaming and driving great gusts through every nook and cranny. "Dear me, I didn't expect anything like this!" exclaims Rupert's Daddy. "It must be coming straight from the Arctic!" Rupert gives a start and remembers Billy Blizzard. "He couldn't . . ." He stops as he hears the faintest of knocks at the front door. He runs to open it and finds Jack Frost hardly able to stand. "Oh, Jack, what's wrong?" Rupert cries as his friend falls into his arms. "It's—Billy—Blizzard," croaks Jack. "He's—escaped!" Rupert pulls his friend into the house and slams the door shut. "Mummy! Daddy! Come quickly, please!" Mr. and Mrs. Bear rush through from the parlour to find Rupert and Jack standing amid the wreckage of the decorations that have been blown down by the wind. "Goodness me!" gasps Mrs. Bear in dismay. "What has happened to him, Rupert?"

RUPERT GETS A NASTY SHOCK

"Billy escaped—not by the door,
He tunnelled through the soft earth floor."

"He's caused this snowstorm, Nutwood's worst!
If only I had trapped him first!"

A gust blows chestsnuts off the grate,
And Daddy cries, "Quick, fetch a plate!"

An icy draught makes Rupert stare.
And Billy Blizzard's gloating there!

Gently Mr. Bear picks Jack up and carries him to an armchair where he soon recovers enough to tell them more. "Billy escaped by digging his way out under the wall of the hut," he says. "I searched day and night but I just couldn't find him. Then he started this blizzard and I couldn't go on any more." Jack sinks back gloomily. "This is going to be the worst weather Nutwood's ever had, you can be sure." Rupert gazes out of the window at the madly swirling snow. "I do wish we could have stopped Billy," he murmurs. "Come on, cheer up!" cries Mr. Bear. "Let's roast some chestnuts!" And soon they are all seated around a roaring fire as chestnuts start to pop on the grate. Then without warning a gust of wind roars down the chimney and scatters the chestnuts. "Fetch a plate, Rupert!" cries Mr. Bear. Rupert starts towards the kitchen, but a sudden bitter blast from the window makes him turn. At the window is a grinning face. Billy Blizzard!

RUPERT TAKES ON AN ADVENTURE

"He's vanished!" "It was him you saw!
We need my cousin, Tommy Thaw!"

"Tommy does not live close at hand,
But far off in volcano land."

"Could Rupert come to help me, please?"
Doubtfully, Mrs Bear agrees.

"Volcano land is right up here.
It's really quite a way, I fear."

By the time the others rush to the window Billy Blizzard has disappeared and there is nothing to see but swirling snow. "Do you know, Billy could keep this going until my other cousin Tommy Thaw decides to come," Jack says anxiously. As they return to the fireside Rupert says, "But couldn't we let Tommy know what's happened?" Jack shakes his head: "It would mean a long journey. He lives in the land of the volcanoes. Besides I should need someone to go with me and help . . . I say, Mrs. Bear, you wouldn't let Rupert come, would you?" Mrs. Bear is taken aback. "I'd look after him all the time?" Jack adds. "Oo, please!" cries Rupert. Mr. Bear looks thoughtful. "Come into my study and show me on the globe where Tommy Thaw lives," he says. Jack studies the globe for a moment then he points to the exact spot. "It seems a very long way for a small bear," muses Rupert's Mummy. "But if you really will look after him, he may go with you."

RUPERT AND JACK SET OFF

"We'll leave tomorrow, that's our plan."
"All right, get all the sleep you can."

Now into bed so snug and warm.
Just listen to that frightful storm!

"Be glad your coat and boots are strong.
You'll need them for the journey's long."

Jack says, "The coldness I don't mind,
But I hate snow-storms of this kind."

Mrs. Bear says that before Rupert and Jack start their journey they must have a good night's sleep. So a bed is made up on the sofa for Jack. Rupert tucks Jack in and the chums excitedly plan their journey until Mummy orders the little bear off to bed. The snow is still swirling thickly and the wind is howling louder than ever as Rupert climbs into bed. Nervously he glances at the window, but there is no sign of Billy. "He would be furious if he knew about our plan," Rupert murmurs.

In the morning Jack is his old cheerful self and he greets Rupert with a smile. "We'll leave right after breakfast," he says. And as soon as they have eaten the friends get ready to go. Rupert's Mummy helps him into rubber boots and his duffel coat. "You're lucky to be able to stand the cold, Jack," he says. "I still hate storms like this," says his friend. But now it is time to leave and Mr. and Mrs. Bear watch anxiously as the pals go out into the fury of the howling blizzard.

RUPERT GOES UP AND AWAY

The snow is thick, the wind is chill.
They stop beneath a rocky hill.

"What! Climb up there?" poor Rupert cries.
"We must! I'll help you," Jack replies.

Jack shouts above the gale, "Hold tight!
We'll wait until the wind's just right."

Then comes a lull. Jack firmly clings
To Ruperts's hand, and off he springs.

Mr. and Mrs. Bear stand by the window and watch Rupert and Jack cross the lane and start up the rising ground. But very soon they lose sight of the two pals in the swirling snow. Above the howl of the wind, Jack shouts, "I'll lead the way!" On they plod for what seems a long time before Jack stops at the bottom of a steep hill and points to its summit. "What? Me? Up there?" gasps Rupert. "We must!" Jack yells. "Come on! I'll help you!" And he guides Rupert up a steep cleft.

Upwards and upwards struggle the pals until at last they reach the top. They can hardly stand upright against the force of the blizzard. "Now," shouts Jack, "hold my hand tightly! Don't let go whatever you do!" "Right!" cries Rupert, clinging to Jack's hand. "As soon as there's a lull in the storm," Jack yells, "we must. . ." Just then there is a drop in the wind. Jack seizes his chance and with Rupert clutching his hand as tightly as he can, shoots up through a gap in the clouds.

RUPERT REACHES VOLCANO LAND

Up through the dark storm clouds they fly,
Emerging into clear blue sky.

Then hand in hand, from danger free,
They cross the wide and shimmering sea.

A line of peaks comes into range.
"Huge smoking chimney pots! How strange!"

Those pots are craters, Rupert's told.
The sand is ash that has turned cold.

With the storm clouds swirling and billowing all around, the pals soar higher and higher. Just as Rupert is beginning to think the clouds will never end he finds himself coming out into bright sunlight. Above them the sky is blue while below a rocky coast stretches into the distance. "Now we must cross the ocean you saw on the globe," Jack calls. "But don't be scared. You're quite safe." Then he tugs Rupert's hand and off they go at a great speed over the wide, shimmering sea.

With the blizzard just a memory the pals fly on and on until at last a line of sunlit peaks looms up. Now the friends begin to lose height slowly. "I can see smoke," says Rupert. "And it's coming from huge chimney pots!" "That's steam," explains Jack. "And those chimney pots are craters. We've reached the land of the volcanoes. Look, all the shore is white with ash!" Now they go skimming low across the beach until Jack sets Rupert down at the foot of one of the volcanoes.

RUPERT STARTS A LONE CLIMB

"It's far too warm for me, I fear,"
Says Jack. "That's why I've brought you here."

Up the volcano Rupert stares.
"Gosh, that's a steep climb!" he declares.

Leaving his duffel coat with Jack,
He starts to climb the rocky stack.

Now nervously he glances round.
"What was that curious hissing sound?"

Rupert is still catching his breath after their thrilling flight when Jack says, "From here you're on your own. It's too warm for someone like me to venture up the crater. That's why I had to bring you. *You'll* have to go and speak to Tommy Thaw." Rupert takes a deep breath. "Right," he says, "I shall do my part now!" But first he takes off his duffel coat. Then he looks up. "I say, it looks pretty steep. I wasn't expecting anything quite like this. Still, here goes!"

Rupert hands his coat to Jack and slowly starts up the steep face of the volcano. There are lots of rocky ledges where he can rest every now and again, but the climb seems endless. At a great height Rupert hears a hissing sound, and looking around sees that he is level with several other craters. Already he is as high as all the other volcanoes and still he has a long way to go to reach the top! "Tommy Thaw *would* have to live in the highest volcano of all!" he mutters.

RUPERT WAKENS TOMMY THAW

He clambers up from ledge to ledge,
Until he's at the crater's edge.

He leans across the ash-strewn wall,
"Hi! Tommy Thaw!" he starts to call.

As through the cloud of steam he peers,
Slow, sleepy footsteps Rupert hears.

"You've come too early! Wait till Spring!
It's too soon to thaw anything."

But still Rupert keeps climbing and soon finds himself on the final stretch. "This part's the worst!" he pants, for now it is really beginning to get warm. As well as the height and the heat, the loud hissing from the crater is frightening. Very cautiously, Rupert clambers the last few feet to the edge of the crater and peers into the great hissing, steaming hole. He can't really see what lies below, but he cups his hands and shouts as loudly as he can, "Tommy Thaw! Are you there?"

There is no answer but the hissing and rumbling from the depths of the crater. Rupert tries again and again. But still no answer. Then he notices a flight of steps going down into the crater. "I wonder if I should go down a little way and call again," he thinks. But before he can decide, a small elf-like creature slowly starts up the steps towards him. "What do you mean disturbing me so early in the season? Please go away, whoever you are, and come back later."

RUPERT ENTERS THE VOLCANO

"Jack said you'd help us. Please don't fail!
It's Billy—" Rupert tells his tale.

"The storm may last for weeks and weeks!"
Rupert grows hotter as he speaks.

"Down here," says Tommy Thaw, "we'll find
Something to change Bill Blizzard's mind!"

"Wait there!" Now Tommy hauls a chain.
"We'll soon get things put right again."

.The little creature is just about to disappear back down the volcano when Rupert leaps on to the crater wall and cries, "Jack Frost sent me!" This stops Tommy Thaw in his tracks. "We badly need your help," Rupert goes on. "Your other cousin, Billy Blizzard has started a terrible snow-storm in Nutwood and he may keep it going until you are due to come and that won't be for weeks and weeks and. . . ." "Oh dear," Tommy says. "I thought Billy was safely banished. H'm, well

there is a way to stop his tricks. Follow me!" Rupert doesn't fancy the idea of going into a volcano but still he follows Tommy down the steps. He is relieved when after a short while they stop beside a big pulley. "Wait there," Tommy calls and reaches for a chain that hangs into the depths of the crater. With much clanking and whirring of gears, Tommy begins to pull something out of the deep hissing hole. "What on earth can it be?" Rupert wonders.

RUPERT GETS A WARM JAR

As Tommy pulls with all his might,
A steaming cauldron comes in sight.

"What are those things? They look like beads
Or even more like glowing seeds!"

"My word, how hot these pellets are!
I feel their glow right through the jar."

Rupert, uncomfortably hot,
Is glad to leave that steamy spot.

Tommy hauls steadily on the clanking chain while Rupert looks on agog. At last he sees something rising from the crater. It is a steaming cauldron at the end of the chain. "Here you are!" Tommy calls cheerfully. Rupert ventures closer as the little creature dips a scoop into the cauldron and brings out some strange bead-like objects. "What are they?" gasps Rupert. "My thaw pellets," Tommy explains. "Just what's needed to deal with that tiresome Billy." Rupert wishes that Tommy would hurry up and explain for he is uncomfortably hot now. Tommy scoops some of the thaw pellets into a strong jar. "There, I've given you more than enough." Rupert can't believe that such little things will stop Billy's mischief. "Still, they must be very strong," he thinks. "I can feel the glow on my hand through the jar." When Tommy has lowered the cauldron again he takes the jar from Rupert. "Up you go, little bear," he says. And they start up the steps.

*"Sprinkle them round him. In two ticks
These pellets will stop Billy's tricks."*

*"Now, on your scarf I'll fix the jar
And tie it tightly. There you are!"*

*"Goodbye, thank you!" And with fresh hope
Rupert starts down the rocky slope.*

*"Hello, Rupert! How did it go?"
Cries Jack who's waiting down below.*

Rupert clambers out of the crater with a great sigh of relief. "It's nice to be in the fresh air again," he pants. "It was really hot down there!" Tommy Thaw puts down the jar he has been carrying. "Tell Jack Frost that this jar contains some of my strongest thaw pellets," he says. "Sprinkle them around Billy Blizzard and they'll soon stop his tricks!" Now Tommy attaches the jar to Rupert's scarf. "Tie this round your waist," he says. "It will be much easier climbing down if your hands are free." Rupert is now ready to leave. "Thank you for helping us, Tommy, and goodbye," he says. Then with the jar of thaw pellets dangling at his waist he sets off down the steep slope. Making his way from ledge to ledge he moves carefully to avoid damaging the jar. At last he sees Jack on the beach below waiting for him. "What happened, Rupert?" he calls as the little bear gets near. "Did you find Tommy?" "Yes, and just see what I have here!" says Rupert.

RUPERT HAS TO FLY AGAIN

"Thaw pellets, Jack! Just feel the heat!
They'll soon end Billy's snow and sleet."

"To King Frost's palace now we go.
Of Billy's tricks he'll have to know."

"Stand on this boulder by my side.
Hold tight!" cries Jack and up they glide.

They streak across the ash white shore
And cross the bright blue sea once more.

Excitedly Rupert unties his scarf from his waist and shows Jack the jar. "Just put your hand near it!" he urges. "It's full of Tommy's strongest thaw pellets. And he says that if we sprinkle a few of them around Billy Blizzard they will soon put a stop to his mischief!" "Oh, splendid!" the other laughs as he feels the glow from the jar of pellets. "Now get ready for another journey," he tells Rupert. "We must go next to King Frost and tell him what has happened." And he points across

the sea in the direction they must take. So once more Rupert puts on his coat and gloves. He picks up the precious jar of thaw pellets in one hand and takes Jack's hand with the other. "Stand on this boulder and hold tight," says Jack. "Now off we go!" He springs into the air lifting Rupert with him. Next moment they are streaking across the beach. This time Rupert is not nervous and he even feels a thrill of excitement as the volcanoes disappear behind them and they fly over the sea.

RUPERT MEETS KING FROST

They spy some battlements at last,
And find a palace, strange and vast.

Though Rupert's glad to reach firm ground,
He glances nervously around.

"A dreadful snow-storm Billy's brought
To Nutwood, Sire! He must be caught!"

"What's this?" the Frost King wants to know.
"It's hot and has a fiery glow."

On and on over the sea fly the two friends and as they go Jack tells Rupert how King Frost just had to banish Billy Blizzard to a distant land for being nasty and troublesome. Now it is much more cold and Rupert is glad of his coat and the warm glow from the jar of thaw pellets. Then suddenly below there are the battlements and turrets of a great castle. "We're here. Get ready to land!" cries Jack and they swoop on to a curved terrace. "Oo, my legs feel wobbly," says Rupert. "It's odd to be on the ground again." But right away Jack leads Rupert to King Frost's icy throne room. The King looks rather stern, thinks Rupert as they bow before him. He looks even sterner when Jack tells him of the blizzard Billy has let loose in Nutwood village. "How dare he defy me!" exclaims the King. "He must be stopped!" Nervously Rupert explains that it was to stop Billy's mischief that he and Jack visited Tommy Thaw. And he shows the King the thaw pellets.

RUPERT AND JACK HEAD HOME

"Thaw pellets, eh? You have *done well!*
Ho, guards!" And King Frost rings a bell.

"Bad Billy Blizzard has returned!
Fetch him! Strict banishment he's earned!"

Says Jack, "We'd best go on ahead."
Then down some stone steps Rupert's led.

At last they reach a spacious ledge,
And Jack Frost stands poised on the edge.

The King becomes less angry as he examines the jar of pellets, but he still looks stern. "You and Jack have done well, little bear," he says as he tugs at a bell-cord by his side. "But we must not delay . . . ah, there you are!" he adds as a pair of armed guards hurry into the throne room. "I am told that Billy Blizzard has left the far place to which I banished him and is now causing trouble in this little bear's village of Nutwood," he says to the guards. "You will don your flying cloaks, fly to Nutwood and recapture him!" As the two guards hurry to obey, Jack leads Rupert from the throne room. "We'll go on ahead," he says. Then he hurries down some steps and across a bridge to a little terrace. "Why do the guards need flying cloaks?" asks Rupert. "Because they don't have my power to fly," Jack explains. He looks around and says, "This seems a good spot for take off. Are you ready?" Rupert, who is becoming quite used to flying, nods. "Then hold tight!" cries Jack.

RUPERT'S CHUM SPOTS TRACKS

Up, up they soar with hands tight clasped,
The jar by Rupert firmly grasped.

Rupert and Jack fly on until
They reach the blizzard raging still.

Still hand in hand they reach the ground.
"Be careful, Rupert, drifts abound!"

"Look, Billy's footprints! There's no doubt!
For no one else would venture out."

"Off we go!" cries Jack, and once again Rupert finds himself whisked into the air. The turrets of King Frost's icy palace are soon left behind as the friends head homeward across the sea. "Now to tackle Billy Blizzard!" cries Jack. "I only hope we can find him!" Rupert hopes so too. Then as they get near home he can see that Billy has not gone. For the great storm clouds still loom over Nutwood as dark and angry as ever. "It really must be awful for the people down there," he thinks as

Jack and he start down through the swirling mass. Down and down they plunge with the icy wind taking their breath away. At last they reach the ground. "Careful! The snow's very deep here," warns Jack as they set off through the blizzard in search of Billy. Once again Rupert is glad of the glow from the jar of pellets. He is just starting to say so when Jack whispers, "Hush!" and points to a line of footprints: "Only one other person would be out in this weather! And that's Billy Blizzard!"

RUPERT AND JACK FIND BILLY

Excitedly the friends press on.
"We'll soon find out where Billy's gone!"

And there is Billy, sure enough,
Chuckling because his storm's so rough.

The friends climb up a snowy groove.
"Let's only hope he doesn't move!"

Rupert gets ready to let go
His pellets on the one below.

With mounting excitement Rupert follows Jack who is tracking the line of footprints. "He can't be far away," says Jack. "Otherwise the snow would have covered up the footprints by this time." At last Jack holds up his hand and halts. The prints have stopped beside a frozen stream between steep banks. The pals peer over the bank. And there is Billy Blizzard breaking icicle darts from a frozen waterfall. "Hee-hee" he sniggers. "I've certainly done my job well. Nutwood's never had such awful weather!" Although Billy's back is turned to the chums Rupert hesitates to go any nearer. "He'll see me if I do," he whispers to Jack. Jack looks about him then beckons Rupert to follow him up a snowy cleft. When they stop they are at the top of the frozen waterfall. Rupert looks over the edge. "He's just below us!" he whispers. As he speaks he opens a slot in the jar. "Then now is your chance!" hisses Jack. "Sprinkle some of the thaw pellets around him!"

RUPERT SPRINKLES THE PELLETS

He shakes the jar and—plop! plop! plop!
Round Billy's feet the pellets drop.

"Oh, no! My lovely blizzard's gone!
A thaw's set in! What's going on?"

Next moment King Frost's guards arrive.
Swish! Through the dwindling storm they dive.

The guards take Billy in their grip.
"Stand still! You shan't give us the slip!"

Billy Blizzard has no idea that his enemies are just over his head and he carries on collecting icicle darts. "Now!" repeats Jack. "Do it now!" Rupert turns the jar upside down and shakes out a stream of glowing thaw pellets. Plop! Plop! Plop! Billy jumps and swings round as the little lumps hit the snow, sizzling and steaming. "Oh, it's a thaw!" he wails. "I'm trapped. My poor lovely blizzard is ruined!" Already Billy's power has gone and as the friends hurry towards the moaning figure the snowstorm starts to fade. Cowering in fear, Billy catches sight of the pals. "Rescue me from this awful thaw!" he whimpers. "You have only yourself to blame," says Jack. "You started the blizzard!" Just then there is a swishing sound and the King's guards swoop from what's left of the storm cloud. "The guards are here!" cries Rupert as they land and make straight for Billy. They grab his arms. "You have defied King Frost!" cries one. "Come with us!"

RUPERT SEES THE SUN RETURN

Jack climbs the slope. "Look, everyone!
The storm has gone! Here comes the sun!"

Then Billy bows his head in shame:
"I'm sorry now. I was to blame!

Billy's whisked off by King Frost's men.
"I doubt he'll trouble us again!"

A cheerful bird starts chirruping,
"Now we can all come out and sing!"

By now the blizzard has died away entirely and the sky is clearing. "Look! The sun is breaking through!" cries Jack joyfully. He and Rupert run to the top of a slope to greet the golden light. "Isn't it peaceful now!" says Rupert. "I'm glad it's all over." Then they return to where Billy stands, weeping and downcast. "I know it was bad of me to start the blizzard. . . ." he begins, but one of the guards breaks in: "No more! It's time to take you to King Frost. He's waiting for you!"

The guards give Jack a smart salute then whisk Billy Blizzard into the air and carry him off to face King Frost. "Will the King be very angry?" Rupert asks. "Well, Billy seems sorry for what he has done so the King might forgive him if he promises to stay where he was banished," Jack says with a shrug. Just then a little bird whistles. Rupert turns. "*You'll* be glad the blizzard has gone," he says. "Oh, yes!" tweets the bird. "We can all come out of shelter and sing again!"

RUPERT SAYS GOODBYE TO JACK

"Although the storm's gone," Jack exclaims,
"There's lots of snow for fun and games!"

"Well, now I must be off," says Jack.
"Goodbye—next winter I'll be back!"

"Have you been helping Jack Frost?"—"Yes!
Our mission was a great success!"

"Pellets? Volcanoes? Old King Frost?"
Rupert's young friends are both quite lost.

Rupert turns to Jack. "It's so calm that it's hard to believe we were struggling through such a blizzard so short a time ago," he says. "Well, it has left lots of snow, so you'll be able to have plenty of fun with your pals," Jack laughs. "And I can promise you that it will last until Tommy Thaw comes in his own good time. By the way, keep the pellets that are left. They might come in handy." So Rupert says goodbye to his good friend Jack and sets off, the jar swinging from his hand. On the slope leading to his cottage Rupert spies two of his chums, Algy and Willie, making a snowman. "I say, we called for you just now," cries Algy, "but your Mummy said you'd gone with Jack Frost to try and stop that awful blizzard." "And we did!" says Rupert, holding up the jar. "With these special thaw pellets from Tommy Thaw's volcano." "Thaw pellets? Volcano? Tommy who?" exclaim his pals. "Oh, I'd better tell you everything!" Rupert laughs.

RUPERT AMAZES HIS DADDY

"You must get home," says Algy, "so
This is the fastest way to go!"

"Hi, Daddy! I've so much to tell!
I'll help to clear that snow as well!"

"Thaw pellets are just what you need.
They melt the thickest snow with speed."

"Do come and look at this, my dear!"
Cries Mr. Bear. "The path's quite clear!"

"... And that's how we stopped the blizzard and got rid of Billy!" Rupert winds up his story. "I say, what an adventure!" cries Algy. "You must be longing to get home. Let's go the quick way, by toboggan!" So with Algy steering, the three pals shoot off downhill. As they tow the toboggan the last few yards they meet Mr. Bear getting ready to clear the snow from his garden path. "Rupert!" he cries. "You're back! We were getting anxious. We've watched for you since the blizzard ended!"

Then Mr. Bear tells Rupert to run and let Mummy know that he's back. "Tell us everything later," he says. But before he goes Rupert hands the jar to Mr. Bear. "Try these pellets, Daddy. If they could stop a snow-storm they should work on your path!" And he scampers indoors leaving his Daddy mystified. When he returns with Mrs. Bear the path is perfectly clear. "Wonderful!" exclaims Daddy. "I sprinkled these pellets and the snow vanished. You do bring home amazing things!"

RUPERT'S MEMORY TEST

Before you try this memory test you must read all the stories in the book. When you have read them study the pictures on this page. Each of them is part of a picture you have seen in one or other of the stories. Then try to answer the questions about them at the bottom of the page. Afterwards check the stories to see if you were right.

1. What happened to shock The Inventor so?
2. What did Tommy haul up from the volcano?
3. Who was on the other side of this door?
4. What job had these sea-horses just done?
5. What place was the walrus pointing to?
6. How had Rupert pleased this little bird?
7. Whose icicle-dart is Jack Frost holding?
8. What magic power had this piece of rod?
9. What unpleasant surprise did Bill get?
10. Who had changed places with this vase?
11. What did Podgy want with these bowls?
12. Who were these guards told to capture?
13. Why was this umbrella so oddly shaped?
14. What is Rupert showing with his roll?
15. What did Bill catch with his new rod?
16. What name is missing from this board?

Page 44. There are eighteen cats besides Dinkie.

Page 45. Algy finds the way.

RUPERT and

It's here at last, the holiday!
And Rupert's come to Shrimpsea Bay!

Shrimpsea Bay! The holiday has really begun! Rupert with his Mummy and Daddy makes his way along the sea-front towards their holiday house. "I'll run ahead and find it!" he laughs. "What is it called?" His Mummy smiles: "'San Remo', like the place in Italy." So Rupert dashes on ahead and soon spies 'San Remo'. "Here it is!" he shouts, pointing with his stick of Shrimpsea rock at a pleasant-looking house.

SHRIMPSEA SAL

the OCEAN OFFICE

*"Ah, there's the house name, large and clear.
Mummy, Daddy, come on! We're here!"*

*"Why, Bill! You're here, too! And what's more,
We shall be living right next door!"*

Then—"Rupert"—a familiar voice rings out, and he turns to find his best pal, Bill Badger. "Bill!" he exclaims. "What. . . ?" Bill chuckles at his amazement and says: "We changed our minds about going to Greyrocks Cove and came here instead. I'm on my way to book a rowing boat for tomorrow. Can you come with me?" Rupert's Mummy who has just come up says that he may, but that the pals mustn't be too long. So off they run.

*"Yes, you may go onto the beach,
But don't stray too far out of reach."*

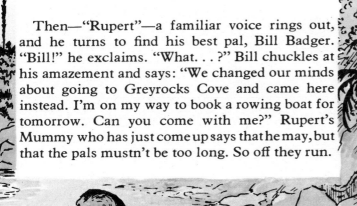

RUPERT AND BILL BOOK A BOAT

"Come on, let's fix up for a row!"
Says Bill, and to the shore they go.

"Whatever are you going to do?"
"Why, fold this little boat in two."

"These boats can't sink! You'll hire one? When?"
Smiles Bill, "Tomorrow morning, then."

Bill laughs. "I'm glad those boats can't sink.
We'll have a super trip, I think."

Rupert and Bill scurry along the sands to where the cliffs begin. "There's where the rowboats are kept!" says Bill pointing to a shed near the edge of the sea. "The man's there. Let's go and fix up a row for tomorrow." As they get near the shed they see that the man is pulling an odd sort of boat out of the water. "Can I do anything for 'ee?" he asks cheerily. But for a moment the two pals are speechless as they watch the man undo some bolts in the middle of the boat then fold the little craft in two. "Never seen a folding boat afore, eh?" chuckles the man. "Mine are all like that. Makes 'em easy to store." "Are they safe?" asks Rupert. "'Course they are!" the man replies. "You just can't sink 'em!" The chums look at each other. "Shall we try one?" Rupert asks. "Yes, let's!" says Bill. So the pals tell the man that they will hire one of his boats next day. Then they hurry back to the sea-front where Mrs. Bear is watching for them from "San Remo".

RUPERT EXPLAINS THE BOAT

"Look!"—Rupert cuts his bread—"Here's how
That rowboat folded up just now."

Smiles Mrs. Bear, "It's time for bed.
You'll be up early, sleepyhead."

"Oh, Bill!" cries Rupert. "This is fine!
Your bedroom's right next door to mine!"

When Rupert wakes the sun is bright.
He bounds from bed with great delight.

At supper Rupert tells his Mummy and Daddy about the odd sort of boat Bill and he plan to take out next day. They look startled when he says that it folds up. But Rupert laughs and tells them how the boat folds, showing them with two pieces of bread. "I say, that *is* a clever idea," agrees Mr. Bear. Later when he is going to bed Rupert asks about something that has been puzzling him. "Why is this house called 'San Remo'?" he asks. "It's an odd sort of name." "Perhaps the owners think it sounds rather nice," Mummy suggests. When Mrs. Bear has gone downstairs Rupert gets up to have one more glimpse of the sea. To his delight he finds that Bill has a room like his in the house next door. "Isn't it nice being neighbours?" Bill laughs. "Well, see you in the morning!" And so the pals go off to sleep at the end of their first day at Shrimpsea. Next day the sun is streaming in when Rupert wakens. He leaps out of bed and bangs on the wall to let Bill know he's up.

RUPERT AND BILL SET TO SEA

"*I've broken up some rock for you.*
There's plenty for your friend Bill, too."

"*Remember, if you lose your way,*
You're from 'San Remo' you must say."

"*Good morning to 'ee and your pal.*
And here's your boat, the 'Shrimpsea Sal'."

"*Keep in the bay for safety's sake.*
Crag rock's the furthest you should make."

Anxious to get off on his boat trip with Bill, Rupert hurries through breakfast. But before he leaves "San Remo" his Daddy gives him a few words of advice about being careful in a boat and his Mummy hands him a paper bag. "I've broken up that stick of rock for you," she says. "Thank you, Mummy," says Rupert, peering into the bag. "Oo! Every piece has 'Shrimpsea Bay' on it!" Then he stuffs the bag in his pocket and hurries off to find Bill. "If you get lost and have to ask the way home, remember you're from 'San Remo'" Mrs. Bear calls after him. The pals reach the boat shed just as the man unfolds one of the little craft and launches it. "'Morning!" he calls to the chums. "Here's your boat—just your size—the 'Shrimpsea Sal'." Rupert sees that the name is painted on the side. Then Bill fetches the oars and the man pushes out the boat. "Don't go beyond yon rock called the Crag," he says pointing out to sea. "The current's strong further out."

RUPERT ROWS TO THE CRAG

The boat is launched and off they go
With Rupert as the first to row.

"You've made it," Bill says with a smile.
"Let's go ashore and rest a while."

Bill takes the rock and smiles, "I say,
Each piece of it reads 'Shrimpsea Bay'!"

Bill glances out to sea. "Oh, my!
I don't like that dark stormy sky."

Rupert takes first turn at rowing. He is a bit clumsy at first but he soon gets used to the feel of the oars and settles down to row steadily. "I must say you're doing well," says Bill. "You've not muffed a single stroke yet." All the time he is pulling towards the rock called the Crag Rupert is remembering what the boatman said about not going beyond it. When at last the boat comes to a gentle stop against the rock Rupert lets out a great sigh: "Whew! My arms are beginning to ache a bit." "Then let's get out and rest for a while and I'll do the rowing when we go back," Bill says. As the pals clamber onto the Crag, Rupert exclaims, "I'm starving. It must be the rowing." Then he remembers the bag of rock in his pocket and pulls it out. "Have a bit, Bill," he offers. "Oo, thanks," says his pal. "I say, every piece has 'Shrimpsea Bay' on it." When they've eaten enough Rupert puts the rest back in his pocket. "Those clouds look stormy," says Bill suddenly.

RUPERT SPIES A GIANT WAVE

"Let's get back quick! The sea's turned rough!
A storm is brewing, sure enough."

Cries Rupert, "Bill, it seems to me
We're being carried out to sea!"

Bill gasps, "I can't row any more."
Just then there comes a frightening roar!

Then with a terrifying sound,
Wild water surges all around!

Rupert doesn't like the look of the darkening sky either. "There's a storm coming, I'm sure," he says. "Come on, Bill. Let's get back at once!" The chums waste no time and soon Bill is pulling strongly towards the land. But all the time the sea is growing rougher. "We're not making much headway in this swell," pants Bill as he struggles to keep his oars in the water. Rupert who has his face towards the land suddenly exclaims in alarm: "We're not getting any nearer the shore! Oh, Bill, we're being carried out to sea!" Bill turns to look at the disappearing land then starts rowing harder than ever. But the little boat is driven further and further out to sea. At last Bill can row no more and droops across the oars. Rupert is just about to take the oars and try when he utters a cry of dismay. A giant crested wave is bearing down on their little craft. Rupert just has time to shout, "Hold tight, Bill!" before the wave is upon them, lifting the boat up and up and up!

RUPERT FINDS HIMSELF ALONE

The water spout's a frightening sight.
Grimly the two chums hang on tight.

When down once more his boat is thrown,
Poor Rupert finds that he's alone!

Though both are safe, the currents start
To pull the two half-boats apart!

As Rupert groans, "What shall I do?"
A tropic isle comes into view.

Desperately the chums cling to their tiny boat as it is swept along at great speed on top of the towering wave. Suddenly the wave begins to sink and Rupert shuts his eyes when he finds himself whirling dizzily downward. There is a bump that sends him sprawling. Then as quickly as it came the great wave is gone leaving Rupert breathless and shaken. "Bill, are you all right?" he calls. There is no answer. Rupert picks himself up and looks around. Bill's half of the boat is gone! Oh, no! Rupert gazes wildly about. But wait! Surely that's it over there. And Bill still has the oars. What's more he has seen Rupert and is shouting, "I'm coming!" What a relief! Then in the same moment Rupert's hopes are dashed. The current is carrying him rapidly away from Bill! Bill's yells grow faint and soon Rupert is alone and dismally wondering if he will ever see home again. Then just when he has almost given up all hope an island comes into view.

RUPERT REACHES AN ISLAND

The boat glides on till Rupert lands
Upon the island's golden sands.

"I only hope that Bill's all right."
But Rupert's pal is not in sight.

"This is the Ocean Office, see?
King Neptune's! For Lost Property!"

"There is the walrus over there,
And he's in charge here, little bear."

To Rupert's joy he finds that the current which took him away from Bill is now carrying him to the island. Soon his half boat is bumping gently on a sandy beach. He jumps out and gazes round him. "Those are palm trees," he murmurs. "And there are so many strange flowers and bushes! Is it a tropical island, I wonder?" Then he remembers Bill and he climbs onto a nearby rock and gazes seaward. But there is not even a speck to be seen on the wide blue ocean.

Suddenly one of the seagulls which have been hovering over the beach swoops and speaks to the little bear. "I suppose you're lost, eh? I don't suppose you'd be here otherwise." Then, seeing Rupert's puzzled look, it adds sharply, "Didn't you know this is the Ocean Office, King Neptune's Lost Property Office?" Rupert shakes his head. "Then you'd better see the walrus!" the seagull squawks. "There he is among the palms." Looking, Rupert makes out a large figure.

RUPERT MEETS THE WALRUS

*"Since he's in charge, the walrus may
Have me sent back to Shrimpsea Bay."*

*Some crabs come past with seaside toys
Lost on the beach by girls and boys.*

*"Well done, hard-working octopus!
You've found the most lost things for us."*

*The walrus grunts, "What's this we've got?
Were you washed up or found or what?"*

The seagull flies off leaving Rupert wondering what it meant about the "Ocean Office" and having to see the walrus. "I suppose the walrus must be in charge of the island," he thinks. "So perhaps I better go and speak to him." He is making his way rather nervously towards the distant figure among the palm trees when a large crab scuttles past him carrying a child's spade and a toy boat. It is followed by other crabs all carrying things in their claws. And they are heading straight for the walrus. Under cover of the bushes, Rupert gets his first good look at the walrus, wearing a uniform and seated at a desk. He sees the crabs hand over their articles to the walrus. They are followed by an octopus carrying several oddments. "Well done!" the walrus tells it. "You must be the hardest working of the sea folk!" When the octopus has gone Rupert steps forward. "Hello," says the walrus, looking up. "How did you arrive here? Were you found or washed up?"

81

RUPERT GIVES HIS ADDRESS

"Ah well, since you have drifted here,
That counts as 'Lost', young bear, I fear."

"You'd be surprised how much we find.
Look. Someone's left a pail behind."

"'Present From Limpet Sands', I learn.
That should be easy to return."

"No—I've no label!" Rupert stares.
"I'm from 'San Remo'," he declares.

Rupert is taken aback by the walrus's question. "Oh, p-please," he stammers, "I drifted here in a boat, or rather half a boat." "Drifted, eh? Then you're lost," grunts the strange creature. "Well, you've certainly come to the right place. This is King Neptune's Lost Property Office. We collect all the things that are lost in the sea. Now I'd like a few particulars . . ." Just then up comes a crab with a seaside pail. "What a busy day this is," says the walrus. "Excuse me while I attend to this."

He takes the pail and examines it all over. "'A Present From Limpet Sands'," he reads out. "Good! No trouble sending this back. Most of the stuff we get here has no clue about where it's come from . . . by the way, do you have a label or something?" Quite bewildered by all that has been happening, Rupert stares back blankly. "I'm sorry, I haven't," he falters. Then he remembers what his Mummy told him before he left. "I-I'm from 'San Remo'," he blurts out.

RUPERT IS NOT UNDERSTOOD

"What's that? San Remo, did he·say?
My goodness, that's a long, long way."

"San Remo? Let's see—here we are!
In Italy! You have come far!"

"So now we know where you must go."
"But it's not that San Remo—no!"

The weary walrus wipes his brow:
"Well, put him in 'UNCLAIMED' for now."

"He's from San Remo! What a distance to have come!" A gabble of astonished cries makes Rupert swing round. Facing him is a collection of odd-looking sea creatures who have been listening to Rupert's words. Even the walrus seems startled at Rupert's words. "San Remo!" he repeats. "It *is* a long way off! Never known such a journey by a piece of lost property. Now, let's see . . ." He crosses to a globe of the world. "San Remo. In Italy if I'm not mistaken. Yes, here it is!" he exclaims. The walrus smiles in a satisfied sort of way. He is clearly pleased with himself. "Right, little bear, we'll soon get you home to Italy." "Italy!" gasps Rupert. "I don't want to go to Italy! I want 'San Remo' in Shrimpsea Bay where my Mummy and Daddy and I are staying!" The walrus passes a flipper wearily across his forehead. "Oh dear!" he sighs. "San Remo in Shrimpsea Bay! This piece of lost property *is* confused. Put it in UNCLAIMED for now."

RUPERT SPIES BILL'S BOAT

"'Lost Pets'," the crab says. "Yes, that's you.
Wait here till we think what to do."

"I wish that they'd pay heed to me . . .
But, wait! There's something out to sea!"

"It's dear old Bill! He is all right!
Hello-o!" shouts Rupert with delight.

A young sea-serpent, swift and strong,
Is pushing Bill's small boat along.

Next thing Rupert knows he is standing beside the dumps where all the lost property is stored. He has been taken there by one of the big crabs which grumbled all the way: "All this prattling about San Remo being in Shrimpsea Bay. You *are* in a fine muddle. Better stay near the sign that says 'Lost Pets' until we decide how we're to get you home to Italy." Then it scuttled away before Rupert could repeat that he didn't want to go to Italy. Suddenly as he is standing there feeling miserable Rupert looks out to sea and notices a speck moving. Hardly daring to hope, he runs to a rock and climbs onto it for a better view. "Oh, yes!" he gasps. "It *is* Bill! But what's that pushing his boat?" Then as his pal's craft draws nearer he sees that it is being propelled by a young sea-serpent. "Hello-ooo there!" he shouts. "I'm here, Bill!" The little boat turns towards Rupert and across the water he hears Bill call, "I'll be right with you, Rupert!"

RUPERT'S PAL TRIES TO HELP

"Oh, Bill, I'm so glad that you've come!"
Cries Rupert as he greets his chum.

He sighs, "No matter what I say,
I can't prove I'm from Shrimpsea Bay."

"My boat can prove it! Look! Its name
Makes plain from Shrimpsea Bay we came!"

"I'll find the walrus and explain,"
Says Bill. "I'll soon be back again."

As Bill's boat nears the shore Rupert runs down to the water's edge to meet him. "Oh, Bill, how glad I am to see you!" he cries as his pal jumps ashore and clasps his hands. "And I'm glad to see *you!*" he laughs. "When we drifted apart I was afraid we'd lost each other for ever. I rowed and rowed without getting anywhere at all. Luckily I was spotted by this young sea-serpent which has pushed me all the way to the island. But I never dreamed I'd find you waiting here. And what sort of place is this?" Excitedly Rupert tells Bill all that has happened to him and about how the walrus wants to send him to Italy. "They don't seem to *want* to understand," he winds up. "If I only had something to prove I'm from Shrimpsea Bay!" Bill frowns. "That's awkward," he muses. "But wait! I can prove we're from Shrimpsea Bay. The name's on my part of the boat!" With rising hopes Rupert tells him where to find the walrus and Bill marches off to put matters right.

RUPERT IS TOLD HE MUST GO

Now Bill returns with gloomy face:
"He's sure you're from that other place."

"San Remo, Italy, he said.
He means to send you there instead!"

"The walrus wouldn't let me tell
Your. . ." CLANG! The crab has rung a bell.

In answer to the bell's command
Sea-horses swim towards the land.

A little later, just after the young sea-serpent has said goodbye and swum back out to sea, Rupert spies Bill returning. His heart sinks for he can see that his chum looks gloomy. "Well, is it all right, Bill?" he asks anxiously. Bill heaves a sigh: "No, it isn't, Rupert. I explained how we were separated. But that walrus didn't even want to understand. He just kept saying that you had told a different story. He's made up his mind you come from San Remo in Italy and that you must go back there!" Rupert gasps in dismay and Bill nods glumly. "It's awful," he agrees. "I'm being sent to Shrimpsea Bay because I have proof that I come from there. But the walrus won't hear of your coming with me. No amount of explaining seemed to make any difference." "Oh dear," quavers Rupert. "What will Mummy and. . ." But Rupert is cut short by the clanging of a bell which is being rung by a crab. Then the chums hear a swishing and turn to see three big sea-horses!

RUPERT AND BILL PART AGAIN

"Into your boat! No time to lose!
San Remo! No, you can't refuse!"

"Oh, please . . ." But Rupert pleads in vain.
The crabs will not let him explain.

"To San Remo in Italy!
Tomorrow you'll be there for tea."

Wistfully Rupert calls, "Goodbye!
Tell Mummy where I've gone and why."

While Rupert and Bill are still wondering what is happening several more crabs appear, all waving their claws excitedly. "Come on, hurry!" urges a big bossy crab as it edges Rupert towards his tiny boat. "You're for San Remo, Italy! Into the boat and we'll harness up the sea-horses!" Meanwhile Bill is having to get his boat ready. In a last attempt to stay with his chum, Rupert pleads: "It really is an awful mistake! My home isn't in Italy! Please let me go back to Shrimpsea Bay!" But like all the other creatures of King Neptune's Lost Property Office the crab doesn't want to pay any attention to Rupert's pleas: "You'll travel first by sea-horse express, then porpoise overnight sleeper then by sea service to San Remo in Italy. You should be there by teatime tomorrow." In no time at all Rupert finds himself being towed out to sea. In despair he calls out to his chum, "G-goodbye, Bill! Please tell my Mummy and Daddy what's happened to me!"

RUPERT REMEMBERS SOMETHING

"Rupert," Bill cries, "goodbye for now!
Be sure we'll get you back somehow!"

The little bear's heart really sinks.
"Oh, what a fix I'm in," he thinks.

He starts up as they gather speed:
"I know the very thing I need!"

"Please take me back without delay!"
The sea-horses at once obey.

"Don't give up, Rupert!" Bill shouts. "We'll get you back somehow. I'll tell your Mummy and Daddy what's happened and . . ." Rupert strains to hear Bill's words as they grow fainter and he is towed away by the team of sea-horses. Faster and faster go the sea-horses while Rupert grows more and more miserable. "Oh dear what a fix I'm in," he sighs. "Goodness only knows when I shall see Mummy and Daddy and Shrimpsea Bay again." Then suddenly, when the island is just a blur on the horizon, Rupert remembers something that jolts him out of his gloom. "It's the very thing! I know it is!" he cries. "It *will* work! It simply has to!" With his hopes beginning to rise again, he shouts to the sea-horses which by this time are fairly racing through the water, "Oh, please, turn back. Take me back to the island!" For a moment Rupert thinks that they are going to ignore him, but then they turn in a wide sweep and with Rupert hanging on tightly head back to the island.

RUPERT RETURNS TO THE ISLAND

He frees the creatures from the boat
And leaves the little craft to float

Then as he glides towards the shore,
He meets his startled pal once more.

"I may convince the walrus now!
My plan's worth trying anyhow."

Says Rupert, "I've some proof for you.
It shows that what I said was true."

As the willing sea-horses pull his boat back to the island, Rupert grows more and more certain that his plan will work. When they enter shallow water he unfastens the tow ropes and sets the sea-horses free. Smoothly his little craft glides to the shore where Bill's boat has been harnessed to another team of sea-horses in readiness for his trip back to Shrimpsea Bay. "Hi, Bill!" Rupert shouts. "Maybe I shan't have to go to Italy after all!" "What's all this?" gasps Bill, dumbfounded.

Rupert leaps ashore and at once is joined by his bewildered chum. "No time to tell you now!" gasps Rupert. "But I'm hoping everything is going to be all right. Come on!" And with Bill at his heels, he dashes to the walrus's Ocean Office. "What! You again!" exclaims the walrus when the little bear rushes up. "I thought we'd dealt with your case." Breathlessly, Rupert explains: "I've come back to show you something!" And from his pocket he takes the rest of his rock.

He shakes the rock lumps out: "That's it!
Look! 'Shrimpsea Bay' on every bit!"

"H'm, where's my magnifying glass?
Yes—'Shrimpsea Bay'—this proof will pass."

"He knows we're both from Shrimpsea Bay
At last!" laughs Bill. "Let's get away!"

The crab says, "If you're being sent
To Shrimpsea Bay, it's time you went!"

Rupert shakes several lumps of his seaside rock onto the walrus's desk. "Please," he begs, "Look at this. Surely this will prove I've come from Shrimpsea Bay!" Bill has arrived by now and he and Rupert hold their breath while, very slowly, the walrus examines the rock through a magnifying glass. After a pause he waggles his whiskers and says, "Yes, I can see the words 'Shrimpsea Bay' quite clearly. It's safe to say you've come from there. It's as good as a label. Why didn't you show me before?" "Because I didn't think of it!" cries Rupert. At once the walrus gives a fresh set of orders to his sea folk for both pals to be taken to Shrimpsea Bay. Rupert and Bill hurry to the shore where Bill bolts the two parts of their boat together again. While he is doing this one of the crabs calls Rupert's attention by snapping its claws. "I hear you're being sent to Shrimpsea Bay now," it says. "Yes, I'm going with my chum," laughs Rupert. "Isn't it wonderful!"

RUPERT AND BILL SPEED HOME

The three sea-horses start to pull
The chums laugh, "This is wonderful!"

"A funny crowd, those Neptune's folk."
"Yes," Bill agrees. "But not a joke."

Cries Rupert, "We're going really fast!
For those were flying fish we passed."

The three slow down in sight of land.
"Now we can row, they understand."

As soon as Bill has fastened the two parts of the boat together securely he shouts to Rupert, "Come on! Aren't you ready to go?" Rupert dashes across to the boat and scrambles aboard, laughing, "Of course, I'm ready, Bill! You don't think I want to stay here any longer, do you?" Then Bill calls to their team of sea-horses and slowly the boat is pulled away from the shore. A group of the sea folk have gathered on the shore to watch the chums go, and as Rupert waves to them he says, "What an odd crowd they are. I don't think that I liked being one of their bits of lost property." Now, as the island disappears the little boat is hauled along at great speed. It even overtakes a school of flying fish. Then at last land comes into view and the sea-horses slow down until the boat comes to a stop. "I think we're there," says Bill. "Yes, this is as far as they'll take us," Rupert agrees. "They know we can row the rest." And he turns the sea-horses loose.

RUPERT'S DADDY IS WAITING

A worried Mr. Bear looks out.
"They're here!" he gives a joyful shout.

The boatman greets them, "My, we're glad
To see you! That there storm was bad!"

"Wait till you hear what we have seen!
And guess where I have nearly been!"

"Now, home! And I'll tell on the way
How Shrimpsea Bay rock saved the day!"

On shore a very worried Mr. Bear is scanning the sea with a pair of powerful glasses. Suddenly, to his great relief, he catches sight of the distant rowboat. "I can see them!" he exclaims. "Yes, I can see both Rupert and Bill!" "That's summat to be thankful for," says the old boatman standing at his side. "I was afeared we might never see them again after that storm." He wades into the water as the boat draws near. "It's good to see you!" he cries. "You had us all mighty anxious!"

As the kindly boatman pulls the boat up onto the slipway, Rupert who is first ashore, runs to his Daddy and throws himself into his arms. "Oh, it's lovely to be back!" he cries. "We've been such a long way! And so much has happened!" Daddy hugs the little bear and swings him off his feet. "I'm sure it has!" he says. "But now you're both safe and sound and you can tell us all about it later." Then Mr. Bear and Rupert and Bill say goodbye to the boatman and go laughing home.

1920
1985